Libby,

You are special!
God loves you!
Adams Apples 1991-92

# Counting
# Katie's Gifts

written by El Louise Price
illustrated by Joe Boddy

Second Printing, 1989
Library of Congress Catalog Card Number 87-91987
©1988. The STANDARD PUBLISHING Company, Cincinnati, Ohio
Division of STANDEX INTERNATIONAL Corporation. Printed in U.S.A.

Katie was happy when she went next door to play with Rhonda. But when she came home, she was about to cry.

"What's the matter, Katie?" her mother asked.

"Rhonda got a present while I was at her house, and I want one too," Katie said, pouting.

"Is it Rhonda's birthday?" Katie's mother asked.

"No," Katie said, shaking her head, "but she got a present anyway. So I want one too. Let's go buy a present for me. OK?"

"I have a better idea," Katie's mother said, reaching for her hand. "Let's go outside and look at some gifts you already have."

Katie agreed. She skipped beside her mother.

"Who gave me the gifts we're going to see?" she asked.

"God did," her mother said.

Katie looked high and low and from side to side. She turned around and looked behind her, too.

"I don't see any gifts," she said.

"You won't find them if you're looking only for things wrapped in bright paper and ribbon," her mother told her.

Katie decided the gifts must be hidden—like Easter eggs. She walked carefully so she wouldn't step on any. Her mother laughed.

"The gifts aren't hidden, Katie. You see some of them every day."

Then Mother whispered softly, "Listen, one of your gifts is singing a beautiful song right now."

Katie stood still and listened. Then she said to her mother, "You're teasing, aren't you, Mother? That's not a gift. That's a bird singing."

Her mother smiled. "I'm not teasing, Katie. Birds are just one of God's gifts to us. See how many more of God's gifts you can find."

Katie decided to hold up a finger for every gift she found.

"Birds," she said, holding up a finger. She looked around.

"Trees. Are trees a gift, too?" she asked. "Help me count please, Mother."

"Yes, trees are a gift from God," her mother said, looking up. "And so is the beautiful sky."

Katie held up two more fingers.

"Did God make clouds, too?"

"Yes," her mother nodded. "And the sun and the moon."

Katie held up two more fingers and a thumb.

"Stars!" Katie said. "God made the stars."

"Oh, yes. And He made the soft, green grass," her mother said, patting the grass.

Katie counted two more fingers.

"Don't forget flowers," Katie said, putting up another finger.

Then she bent down to smell the flowers and something jumped out at her.

"Oh," Katie said, jumping back. Then she saw it was a grasshopper.

"Are grasshoppers a gift?" she asked, laughing.

Katie's mother laughed, too.

"Grasshoppers are a funny gift, aren't they? But be sure to count them," she said. "And bugs and bees. God made them all."

Katie looked at her hands and sighed. "Why did God give me so many gifts?"

"Because He loves you so much," her mother said.

"But I can't count them all. God has given me so many gifts," Katie said, "I've run out of fingers."

"Maybe you can count them on your toes then," her mother suggested, laughing.

Katie started to pull off her shoes. Then she laughed, too, and rolled over in the grass.

"That's a funny joke, Mother," she said.

Katie's mother thought it was funny, too. She knew that even counting on her toes, Katie could never count all of God's wonderful gifts.